THE SPELL OF A STORY

MARIAJO ILUSTRAJO

TO MY SISTERS, WHO SHOWED ME
THE POWER OF READING.
M.I.

First Published in 2024 by Frances Lincoln Children's Books,
an imprint of The Quarto Group.
100 Cummings Center, Suite 265D, Beverly, MA 01915, USA.
T +1 978-282-9590 F +1 078-283-2742 www.Quarto.com

A catalogue record for this book is available from the British Library.

ISBN 978-0-7112-7801-1
E-ISBN 978-0-7112-7800-4

The illustrations were created in acrylic gouache, ink and colour pencils
Set in Mariajo

Published by Peter Marley
Designed by Karissa Santos
Commissioned and edited by Lucy Brownridge
Production by Dawn Cameron

Manufactured in Guangdong, China TT112023

9 8 7 6 5 4 3 2 1

THE SPELL OF A STORY

MARIAJO ILUSTRAJO

Frances Lincoln
Children's Books

FINALLY, IT'S THE LAST DAY OF SCHOOL.
THAT MEANS NO MORE WAKING UP EARLY,
NO MORE POP QUIZZES, AND MOST IMPORTANTLY...
NO MORE READING.

A WHOLE BOOK?

BUT i HATE BOOKS.

WOW, THEY LOOK EVEN MORE BORING WHEN THEY'RE ALL TOGETHER. HOW DO YOU CHOOSE? THEY'RE ALL JUST QUIET AND STILL.

I REALLY DON'T KNOW WHERE TO BEGIN.

ABSOLUTELY NOT THAT ONE.

NOT THIS ONE EITHER. A MERMAID WHO WANTS TO BECOME HUMAN BECAUSE OF A HANDSOME... PRINCE?

PUUUURLEASE.

NO, THANKS!

RETURNS

AT HOME THE BOOK LOOKS EVEN BIGGER.
THIS IS THE LONGEST BOOK THAT EVER EXISTED!
WHAT WAS SHE THINKING? IT WILL TAKE ME ALL SUMMER...

I SUPPOSE I SHOULD BEGIN AT THE BEGINNING.

THIS IS ACTUALLY NOT A BAD START.

I GUESS IT COULD BE WO...

What am I wearing?

And... who are you?

Hi! Are you ready?

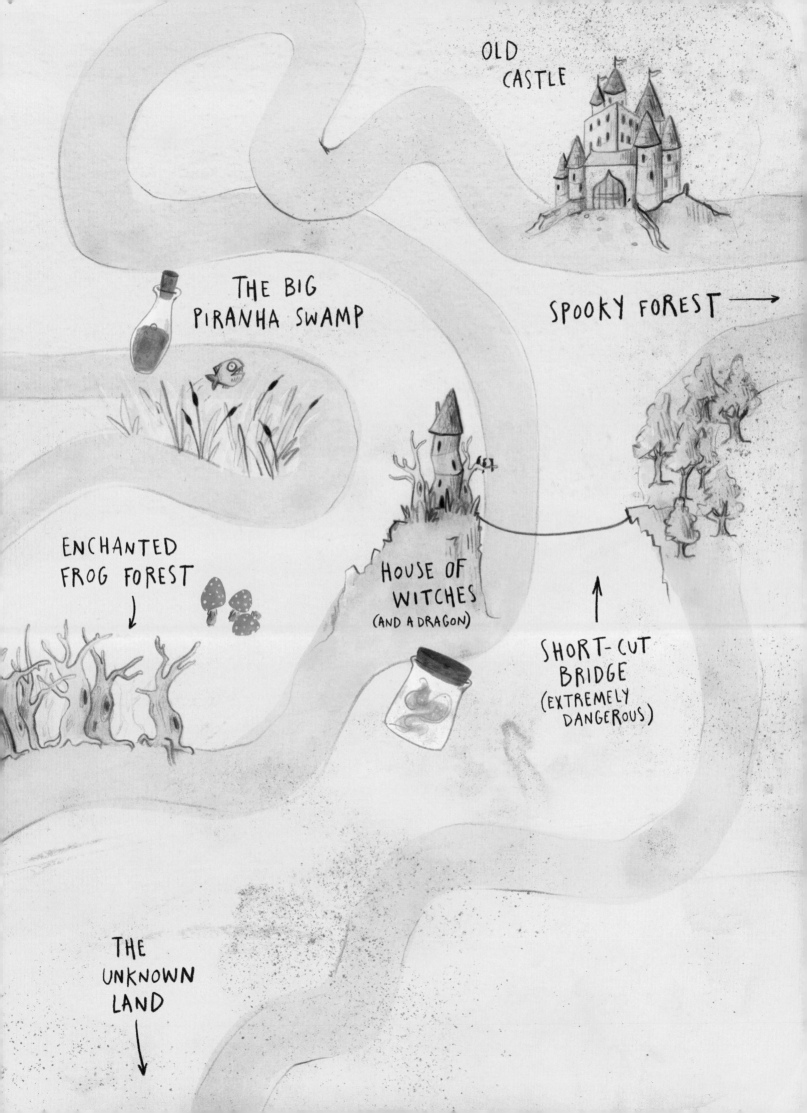

OLD CASTLE

THE BIG PIRANHA SWAMP

SPOOKY FOREST →

ENCHANTED FROG FOREST ↓

HOUSE OF WITCHES (AND A DRAGON)

SHORT-CUT BRIDGE (EXTREMELY DANGEROUS) ↑

THE UNKNOWN LAND ↓

... and **scary** places!

We'll battle naughty pirates,

dance with
enchanted frogs,

And you'll have tea with mischievous witches.
After all, someone has to distract them while
I find the last ingredient...

I EAT,

I thought you hated reading?

TAKE A BATH,

AND BRUSH MY TEETH AS FAST AS I CAN.

I NEED TO KNOW HOW THIS ENDS.

WHERE WAS I?

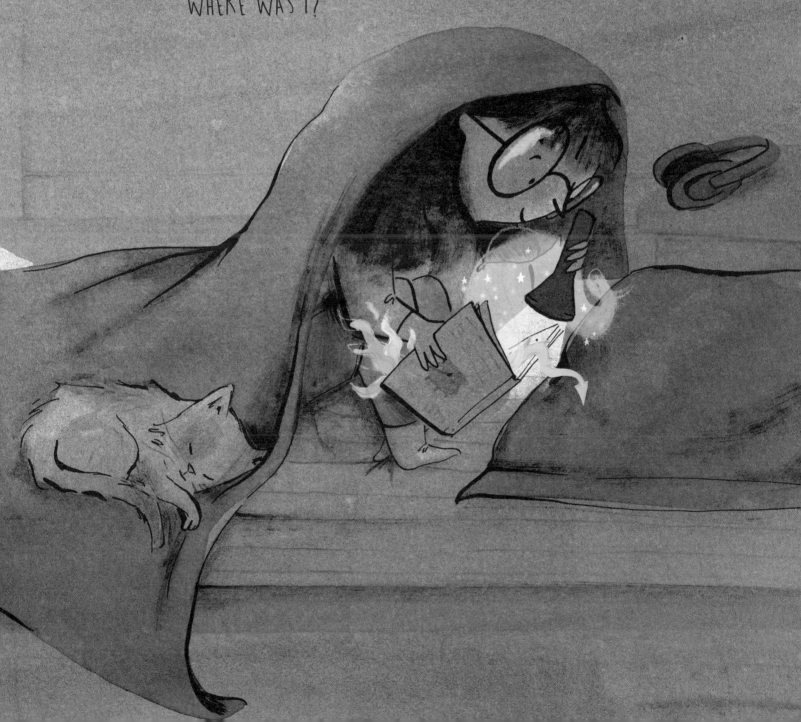

BACK IN THE STORY, THE DRAGON DOESN'T
SEEM HAPPY THAT WE'VE "BORROWED" THE
POTION HE WAS GUARDING. HE IS FOLLOWING US,
WHICH I DON'T THINK WAS PART OF THE PLAN!

HOUSE OF
WITCHES
(AND A DRAGON)

SHORT-CUT
BRIDGE
(EXTREMELY
DANGEROUS)

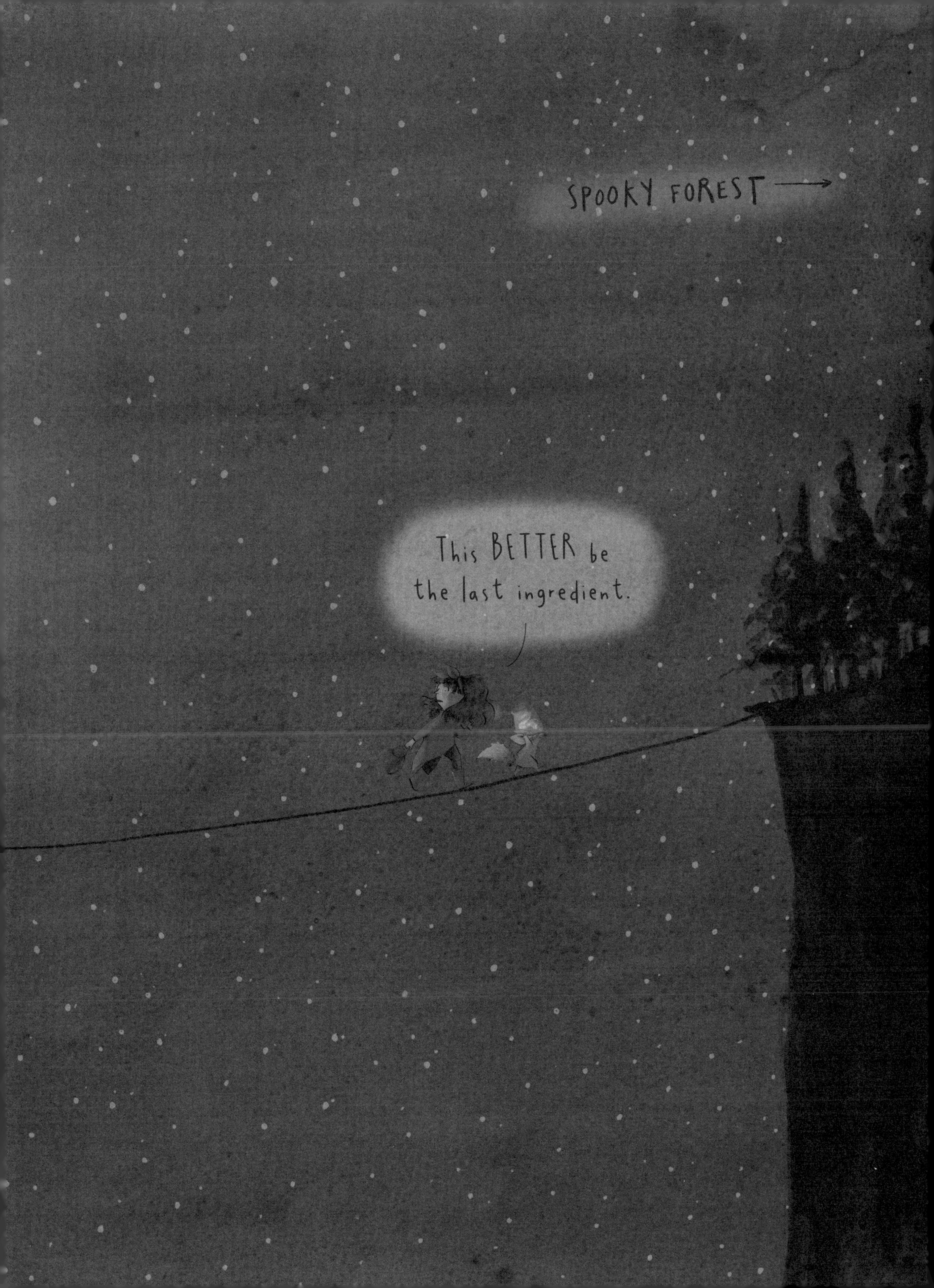
SPOOKY FOREST →
This BETTER be the last ingredient.

I think we have everything we need for me to cast my spell! Let's see, now.

Oh, yes! Let's not forget the
most important ingredient...

One of my hairs?
Are you finally going to tell me
why we need all of these things?

Now, we just...

need to do a little...

MAGIC!

Repeat after me...

Pickled lettuce,

PICKLED LETTUCE,

dancing tree,

DANCING TREE,

cast this powerful

CAST THIS POWERFUL

spell for me!

SPELL FOR ME!

Oh good, the potion worked, the spell is cast!

What happened?

Can't you tell? You're completely different. You've fallen under the most powerful of spells: the spell of a story.

I suppose I do feel very different.

Well, of course you do.

And just like that, I was transformed, into a story adventurer.